ALICE FAYE
DUNCAN

YELLOW
DOG
BLUES

CHRIS
RASCHKA

EERDMANS BOOKS FOR YOUNG READERS

GRAND RAPIDS, MICHIGAN

Text © 2022 Alice Faye Duncan
Illustrations © 2022 Chris Raschka

Published in 2022 by
Eerdmans Books for Young Readers,
an imprint of Wm. B. Eerdmans Publishing Co.
Grand Rapids, Michigan

www.eerdmans.com/youngreaders

Manufactured in the United States of America

31 30 29 28 27 26 25 24 23 22    1 2 3 4 5 6 7 8 9

A catalog record of this book is available from the Library of Congress

Illustrations created with fabric paint and embroidery thread on raw canvas

I woke up early one morning before the light of day. I fixed my dog a big pot of bones and breakfast scraps.

Sometimes life is a mystery. Love is a mountain climb. The blues grabbed me like a shaking chill. I found my dog house—empty.

**"YELLOW DOG,"**

I hollered, with tears welling up my eyes. The rusty gate swung back and forth.

My puppy love

. . . was gone.

I crossed the road
and asked Farmer Fred,
"Did Yellow Dog pass this way?"

"Bo Willie," he replied
as he fed his spotted mule,
"Old Yella hit Highway 61.

I ran toward Cleveland on 61
and searched behind
the grocery store.
I searched around
the garbage bin
and beneath the
grocery porch.

"NO DOG HERE,"

called Mr. Yee, dressed
in his store apron.
His wife pointed north.
Yee Junior brightly
chimed in: "I saw that
dog on Dockery Farm,

I hiked my heels toward Dockery—but did not see a soul. All I found was a faded sign painted in big letters. It said,

"MISSISSIPPI BOOGIE! VISIT MERIGOLD!"

I raised my thumb
and hitched a ride.
Merigold was far away.
It was much too far to walk
or run in the Mississippi heat.
Aunt Jessie saw me on the road
and stopped her Cadillac.
Then we drove toward Merigold
to shimmy, shake, and boogie.

While Aunt Jessie and Mr. Willie
danced under the disco lights,
I searched the crowded club
for my missing puppy love.
He did not show up in
Merigold, and my tears
broke like a river.

Aunt Jessie said, "You better
not stain my velvet seats."
Like a patient saint, she took
her flower handkerchief and
cleaned my snotty nose.

I cried like a baby—
"Let's leave this
juke joint town."

Mr. Willie waved goodbye while chomping on a fat cigar.

We moseyed up the crossroads
to Highway 8 and 1.

"YELLOW DOG,"

I hollered across the
lonesome road. Yellow Dog
was nowhere in sight.
The dog had come
and gone.

Aunt Jessie's good luck charm wasn't bringing us no success. She got herself to thinking hard and followed common sense. She parked her Caddy in Clarksdale at the Hicks' tamale stand.

TAMALES

HICKS

A man on a corner gave a wild report like something we never heard.

He said, "I saw a yellow dog. That scamp left here on a Greyhound bus.

A BAND?
Aunt Jessie hollered to the heavens, "Where can that little dog be?"

I studied the map across my lap, and the answer looked back at me.

Yellow Dog moved to Memphis!
He followed the city lights.
He sings the blues on
Beale Street now.
He sings all day and night.

SOME DOGS ARE
VERY FAITHFUL.
THEY WILL NEVER
LEAVE YOUR SIDE.

SOME DOGS RAMBLE
AND RUN THE ROAD.
THEY LOVE YOU AND THEN
THEY'RE GONE.

What is the moral
to this story?
What is the lesson
to this tale?

# DELTA BLUES
*How the Music Was Born*

The Mississippi Delta lies between the Yazoo and Mississippi rivers in the northwest corner of the state. During the early 1800s, before the Civil War, white land developers settled in the fertile flood region. They raised cotton plantations that thrived on the backs of Blacks who were enslaved labor. When slavery was abolished, some white planters formed economic structures that robbed earnings from the Black families hired on the land as sharecroppers or tenant farmers. Out of these spirit-breaking systems of injustice during and after slavery, Black Americans gave birth to blues music.

"Delta blues" is a genre of acoustic music that was formed in the belly of the Mississippi Delta region. Blues musicians played guitars, banjos, harmonicas, fifes, drums, and one-string diddley bows tacked to the side of cropper shacks. Some Black workers turned these homes and other abandoned buildings into juke joints—gathering places where Black people could relax with food, drinks, music, and dancing.

Burdened by the weariness of segregation, unprofitable farming, and terror associated with lynching in the early twentieth century, Delta blues musicians created riveting sounds. While most lyrics in the music speak of loss, loneliness, and suffering, Delta blues music of the past and the present also provides listeners with dancing pleasure, soul reflection, and thrilling joy.

# YELLOW DOG BLUES

*A Music Journey through
the Mississippi Delta*

As Bo Willie hits the road to find his pet, he visits seven sites that are important to American music and to what historians call the "Mississippi Blues Trail." Blues greats like B.B. King, John Lee Hooker, and Muddy Waters were born in the Delta and were shaped by its sights and sounds. The musicians eventually moved north to big cities such as Chicago, Detroit, and New York during the Great Migration of the 1940s. The migration of Delta blues transformed the music into an electric sound, which gave birth to rock and roll. Here in this book, you can travel the Mississippi Blues Trail with Bo Willie as he seeks to find his runaway hound.

## Highway 61
Part of this winding highway snakes up through the Mississippi Delta into Memphis, Tennessee. The Delta section is called the "Blues Trail" because many blues musicians were born in the area.

## Dockery Plantation
This is the cotton plantation where famous musicians like Charley Patton, Robert Johnson, and Muddy Waters learned to play the blues guitar.

## Merigold Blues Club
This blues club in Merigold, Mississippi, was one of the last plantation juke joints in the United States. Known as "Po' Monkey's Lounge," it was operated by Willie "Po' Monkey" Seaberry, who died in 2016.

## Crossroads

Southern folklore says Robert Johnson sold his soul to the devil in exchange for the power to play blues guitar. The exchange is said to have happened in several places. One alleged site is Rosedale, Mississippi, where Highway 8 crosses Highway 1.

## Hicks' Tamales

The Delta is famous for blues music and hot tamales, a Mexican specialty. Travelers visit Clarksdale, Mississippi, to speak with chef Eugene Hicks and enjoy his secret tamale recipe.

## Memphis, Tennessee

Called the "front door of the Delta," Memphis is a city where Black artists continue to create innovative traditions in gospel, blues, jazz, and soul music. Father of the Blues W.C. Handy wrote his most popular blues tunes while living in Memphis.

## Beale Street

This famous Memphis street bustled with music in the early 1900s—and still does to this day. Delta guitarists like B.B. King played on Beale to develop their skills. B.B. King went on to be crowned America's "King of the Blues."